Dear Parents and Educators,

Welcome to Penguin Young Readers! As parents and educators, you know that each child develops at his or her own pace—in terms of speech, critical thinking, and, of course, reading. Penguin Young Readers recognizes this fact. As a result, each Penguin Young Readers book is assigned a traditional easy-to-read level (1–4) as well as a Guided Reading Level (A–P). Both of these systems will help you choose the right book for your child. Please refer to the back of each book for specific leveling information. Penguin Young Readers features esteemed authors and illustrators, stories about favorite characters, fascinating nonfiction, and more!

Froggy Is the Best

LEVEL **2**

GUIDED READING LEVEL **I**

This book is perfect for a **Progressing Reader** who:
- can figure out unknown words by using picture and context clues;
- can recognize beginning, middle, and ending sounds;
- can make and confirm predictions about what will happen in the text; and
- can distinguish between fiction and nonfiction.

Here are some **activities** you can do during and after reading this book:
- Picture Clues: Use the pictures to tell the story. Have the child go through the book, retelling the story just by looking at the pictures.
- Make Connections: Froggy tries many activities in order to figure out what he is the best at. Discuss your favorite activities. What are you the best at?

Remember, sharing the love of reading with a child is the best gift you can give!

—Bonnie Bader, EdM
   Penguin Young Readers program

*Penguin Young Readers are leveled by independent reviewers applying the standards developed by Irene Fountas and Gay Su Pinnell in *Matching Books to Readers: Using Leveled Books in Guided Reading*, Heinemann, 1999.

For Aaron and Sean and my best wife,
Maureen, and for Annika and Mattias—JL

For Minju, also among The Best—FR

PENGUIN YOUNG READERS
Published by the Penguin Group
Penguin Group (USA) LLC, 375 Hudson Street, New York, New York 10014, USA

USA | Canada | UK | Ireland | Australia | New Zealand | India | South Africa | China

penguin.com
A Penguin Random House Company

Text copyright © 2015 by Jonathan London. Illustrations copyright © 1995, 1998, 1999, 2000,
2002, 2003, 2004, 2006, 2007, 2008, 2011 by Frank Remkiewicz. All rights reserved. Published in 2015
by Penguin Young Readers, an imprint of Penguin Group (USA) LLC, 345 Hudson Street,
New York, New York 10014. Manufactured in China.

Library of Congress Cataloging-in-Publication Data is available.

ISBN 978-0-448-48380-1 (pbk)   10 9 8 7 6 5 4 3 2 1
ISBN 978-0-448-48381-8 (hc)   10 9 8 7 6 5 4 3 2 1

FROGGY

IS THE BEST

by Jonathan London
illustrated by Frank Remkiewicz

Penguin Young Readers
An Imprint of Penguin Group (USA) LLC

Froggy woke up

and jumped on his bed—

boing! boing! boing!

"I feel good!" he said to himself.

"I am the best!"

But what was Froggy the best at?

"FRROOGGYY!" called his dad.

"Wha-a-a-t?" cried Froggy.

"It's time to eat!"

So Froggy hopped out of bed

and got dressed.

He pulled on his underwear—

zap!

He pulled on his shorts—*zip!*

He pulled on his shirt—*zim!*

He pulled on his socks—*zoop!*

And he pulled on his sneakers—

zup!

Then he flopped to the kitchen—

flop, flop, flop.

And he ate his bowl of cereal

and flies—*munch, crunch, munch.*

"I feel good!" he said to himself.

"I am the best!

But what am I the best at?"

After eating, he sat under the table and had a daydream about what he was best at.

"Am I the best at swimming?"

Splash!

No.

"Am I the best at golf?"

Bam! Bam! Bam! Bonk!

No!

"Am I the best at riding a bike?"

Zoom!

No!

15

"Am I the best at baking a cake?"

No!

"Am I the best at playing T-ball?"

Swat!

No!

"Am I the best at playing

tetherball?"

Bonk!

No!

"Am I the best at playing

the saxophone?"

Honk!

No!

"Am I the best at using

a bow and arrow?"

Zap!

No!

"Am I the best at kayaking?"

Splash!

No!

"Am I the best at surfing?"

Wipe out!

No!

"Am I the best at playing soccer?"

"Save!" shouted Froggy,

holding the ball.

But he was not the goalie.

"Oops!" cried Froggy,
looking more red in the face
than green.

So what was Froggy the best at?

He hopped up and hit his head

on the table—*bonk!*

He flopped outside—*flop, flop, flop.*